SEVEN SILLIES

Written by Joyce Dunbar

Illustrated by Chris Downing

RED FOX

On a bright and shining morning Pig looked into the pond.

"There's a pig in the pond," said Pig.
"Such a handsome pig!"
And Pig called over to Sheep.

"What do you see in the pond?" asked Pig.
"I see a pig and a sheep," answered Sheep.
"Such a beautiful sheep!"
And Sheep called over to Goat.

"What do you see in the pond?" asked Sheep.
"I see a pig and a sheep and a goat," answered
Goat.
"Such a gorgeous goat."
And Goat called over to Rabbit.

"What do you see in the pond?" asked Goat.
"I see a pig and a sheep and a goat and a rabbit,"
answered Rabbit.
"Such a splendid rabbit!"
And Rabbit called over to Hen.

"What do you see in the pond?" asked Rabbit.
"I see a pig and a sheep and a goat and a rabbit and a hen," said Hen.
"Such a fine feathered hen."
And Hen called over to Mouse.

"What do you see in the pond?" asked Hen.
"I see a pig and a sheep and a goat and a
rabbit and a hen and a mouse," said Mouse.
"Such a dear little mouse."
And Mouse called over to Frog.

"What do you see in the pond?" asked Mouse.
"I see seven sillies," answered Frog.
"Seven sillies?" asked the pig and the sheep
and the goat and the rabbit and the hen and
the mouse. "What do you mean?"

"They are all in the pond and they want to get out," said Frog.
"How can we get them out?"
"You will have to jump in and fetch them," answered Frog.

So the pig and the sheep and the goat and the rabbit and the hen and the mouse all jumped into the water with a splash!

"There is nothing in the pond after all!" they said.

"Oh yes there is," laughed Frog.
"There is a handsome pig,
a beautiful sheep,
a gorgeous goat,
a splendid rabbit,
a fine feathered hen,
a dear little mouse,
and that makes seven sillies."

The animals scrambled out of the pond all sopping and dripping with water. They did feel very silly!
"How many sillies?" asked Pig.

"Seven," answered Frog.
"Are you sure?" asked Pig.
Pig began to count. The animals joined in.
"One, two, three, four, five, six —"
The only one left was Frog.
"Aha!" they laughed. "SEVEN SILLIES!"

"We see a frog that can't count," they said.
"Such a foolish frog!"

For John & Kate Tremain - J.D.
For Caroline, Chloë and Max - C.D.

A Red Fox Book
Published by Random House Children's Books
20 Vauxhall Bridge Road, London SW1V 2SA
A division of The Random House Group Ltd
London Melbourne Sydney Auckland
Johannesburg and agencies throughout the world

Copyright text © Joyce Dunbar 1993
Copyright illustrations © Chris Downing 1993

1 3 5 7 9 10 8 6 4 2

First published in Great Britain by Andersen Press 1993
Red Fox edition 1999

Printed in Singapore

The Random House Group Reg. No. 954009
www.randomhouse.co.uk

ISBN 0 09 187308 8